Bless Your Heart

Holly Bea

Illustrated by Kim Howard

H J Kramer
Starseed Press
Tiburon, California

Art Director: Linda Kramer
Design and Production: Jan Phillips, San Anselmo, California

Library of Congress Cataloging-in-Publication Data

Bea, Holly, 1956-
   Bless your heart / Holly Bea ; illustrated by Kim Howard.
   p. cm.
   Summary: In bedtime prayers, children bless all sorts of things, from hugs and birds to
friends and chores.
   ISBN 0-915811-94-4 (cloth : alk. paper)
   [I. Prayers—Fiction. 2. Bedtime—Fiction. 3. Stories in rhyme.] I.Howard, Kim, ill. II.
Title.

PZ8.3.B3485 B1 2001
[E]—dc2l
                                                                              00-069538

H J Kramer Inc
Starseed Press
P.O. Box 1082
Tiburon, California 94920
Printed in Singapore
10 9 8 7 6 5 4 3 2

In memory of my teacher, Lina Jean Davis, and to all
educators who change the
course of our lives.
H. B.

For Wilma Connor and her family who have stood by
my side through every smile and tear in
the last twenty-five years. Bless
your hearts always.
K. H.

Bless the early morning light.

Bless your eyes so shiny bright.

Bless the hug you give to me.
Bless the freckle on your knee.

Bless the way you say hello.
Bless the knot, and bless the bow.

Bless your giggle, bless your cry.
Bless the way you say good-bye.

Bless the fun you'll have today.
Bless your friends along the way.

Bless your busy little hands.
Bless your castles made of sand.

Bless the shells, and bless the star.
Bless exactly who you are.

Bless your boo-boo and your tears.
Bless your tiny little ears.

Bless the tidepools and the birds.
Bless your kind and gentle words.

Bless your legs so fast and strong.
Bless the path you travel on.

Bless your silence and your song.
Bless the place where you belong.

Bless the chores that you will do.
Bless you when you say "Ahh-choo!"

Bless your fingers and your toes.
Bless your little button nose.

Bless your special inner Light.
Say a prayer and bless this night.

Bless your heart, you are the best.
Now bless my soul, it's time to rest!